ATTILA
THE
PUN

The Other Magic Moscow Book
The Magic Moscow

ATTILA THE PUN

A Magic Moscow Story

Daniel Pinkwater

Aladdin Paperbacks

First Aladdin Paperbacks edition 1995
Copyright © 1981 by Daniel Pinkwater
All rights reserved, including the right of reproduction in whole or in part
in any form

Aladdin Paperbacks
An imprint of Simon & Schuster Children's Publishing Division
1230 Avenue of the Americas
New York, NY 10020
Printed in the United States of America
10 9 8 7 6 5 4 3 2 1

Library of Congress Cataloging-in-Publication Data
Pinkwater, Daniel Manus, date.
    Attila the Pun : a Magic Moscow story / Daniel Pinkwater. — 1st
  Aladdin Paperbacks ed.
            p.   cm.
    Summary: When the mystic seer of Hoboken and the employees of
  the Magic Moscow summon the ghost of a famous person, they get a
  punster with a collection of 1500-year-old jokes.
    ISBN 0-689-71764-4
    [1. Puns and punning—Fiction.   2. Ghosts—Fiction.   3. Humorous
  stories.]   I. Title.
PZ7.P6335At   1995
[Fic]—dc20   94-468

To
the Members
of the
Hoi Polloi Club

"SEMEL
  INSANIVIMUS
  OMNES"

Any resemblance
to persons living or dead
is purely coincidental.

ATTILA THE PUN

A Magic Moscow Story

ONE

OBODY HAS A ROOM like mine. It's the whole basement of our house on River Street. A long time ago, before we lived in the house, somebody made the basement into a sort of indoor beer garden, with paintings on all the walls. Actually, it's just one painting that goes all around the walls—a mural. It shows green hills, lakes with sailboats, trees and flowers, and lots of grapevines.

There are little light fixtures in the ceiling, covered with pieces of colored glass. There is a panel with ten switches to control the lights. You can get all red lights, or red and blue, or blue and green. The mural looks really good with the blue-and-green-colored lights on.

At one end of my basement, there's a bar. I made that into my desk. I just pulled one of the tall stools behind the bar and put my lamp on it—and there was my desk. There are plenty of shelves behind the bar and under it. It makes a great place to write and do homework. And, get this, there's a little tiny refrigerator under the bar, where I can keep cold orange juice and stuff.

Of course, there isn't a whole lot of daylight in my room. All that gets through the four little windows up near the ceiling is enough to make the mural look like twilight in the forest. That doesn't bother me; if I want sunshine, I can go outside. If I drag one of the barstools up to one of the little windows, I can crawl out. Of course, I can just go up the stairs and out the front door too—but I can sneak out the window without anybody knowing it.

The best thing about my room is its size. I have room for just about anything. If I find something, no matter how big it is, I can take it back to my room. For example, I have an actual stuffed moose head. That's something I found. It had one antler broken off. I dragged it home and wrapped the broken antler with friction tape. It sags a little, but the moose head still looks great.

Another thing I found was an old-time record player. It's the kind you wind with a crank. It's on wheels, so I rolled it home. The whole thing is about as tall as me, and there's a sort of cabinet in front. I found a bunch of really old records in it.

The record player didn't work at first, but I squirted some oil here and there, and now it works fine.

It's amazing what you can find on the street in Hoboken. You just have to keep a sharp lookout— and have someplace to take what you find.

I have a family, of course, but they don't come down to my room much. My mother says it's disgusting. She doesn't like the moose head: She says it must have fleas. I am responsible for my own cleaning and I keep the room nice. I don't care what my mother says.

3

It's just my mother and father and me at home. I have a married sister. She lives in Idaho, on a farm with a lot of other people. It's a communal farm, which means they all work together and share everything. She calls home once in a while to ask for money. Her husband is sort of a neat guy. His name is Ron. They have three kids named Sun, Moon, and Beancurd. Once a year they all visit us. They're relaxing people to have around. They meditate. My father says they're harmless.

My sister's name is Louise. She's okay. I also have an older brother. His name is Neil. I'm sorry to say, Neil is a jerk. He thinks he's wonderful. I don't know why. When Neil comes home, he always wants to go out in the street and throw a ball back and forth with me. This goes on for about fifteen minutes. The rest of the time he ignores me. Neil and Louise are both a good deal older than me; we haven't got much in common.

I have a cat named Arthur. Arthur is strictly *my* cat. There's nobody else he likes. Arthur happens to be one of the smartest cats in history. He comes and goes through one of the windows. He's orange, and he has bad breath. He's an outstanding cat. He really likes me. He also likes the old jazz records I found with the windup record player. When I play them, Arthur rubs against the legs of the machine. Arthur's favorite record—and mine—is called "West End Blues" by Louis Armstrong.

4

TWO

SOMEONE ELSE WHO likes old records is Steve Nickelson. Steve is my friend. He is also my boss. He runs the Magic Moscow.

The Magic Moscow is mainly an ice-cream stand—but Steve also sells hamburgers, carrot juice, and bean-sprout salad. Steve is divided in his love for health food and fattening junk.

Steve collects comic books, old records, pennies, bottle caps, antique sneakers, and all sorts of things. He also has a dog named Edward who lives in the Magic Moscow, since Steve's parents won't let him in their house.

My part-time job is helping Steve in the Magic Moscow, but sometimes I get to help him with his collections. We both take care of Edward.

In the summer, I work full time for Steve. My parents say I don't have to do that. They say I could go to camp or just hang out with the other

kids, but I'd rather work. During the school term, when I'm only working part time, I'm always afraid I'll miss something at the Magic Moscow. All sorts of interesting things happen and all sorts of interesting people come in while I'm in school.

In the summer, I'm at the Magic Moscow from the time it opens until the time it closes—that's thirteen hours a day—so I don't miss a thing.

I also make huge sums of money working all those hours. I think there's a law that says a kid can't work more than eight hours, but I do anyway. Of course, Steve lets me goof off any time I want to. I can go into the restaurant part of the Magic Moscow and sit around and read, or talk to my friends. The restaurant part of the Magic Moscow used to be a parking lot. Then he put a roof over it and set up picnic tables; next he put walls around it—and it became a restaurant. I helped Steve put posters and comic book covers up all around the walls. After my room, it's the neatest place in town.

THREE

ONE TIME, STEVE LEFT me in charge of the Magic Moscow, while he went to see about buying some telephones. He had taken to buying up all sorts of telephones, old and new. Another collection.

I had run the Magic Moscow all by myself lots of times. In the evening, Steve would close up the restaurant and turn off the grill. Then we'd just sell ice cream through the little window to people in the street.

It was a cool evening. There wouldn't be a lot of business. I could handle it. Steve had left a stack of Django Reinhardt records behind the counter, and I was playing them on the old phonograph he keeps in the store.

A couple of kids came by for one-scoop cones with sprinkles, and a family pulled up in a car, all wanting strawberry milkshakes. Easy.

For a long time, nobody came. Nobody even passed by. I sat on a stool near the little window, listening to Django and leafing through an old copy of *Stupefying Science Fiction*. The Magic Moscow has these yellow fluorescent lights. They're supposed to repel bugs, but what they really do is make it impossible to enjoy comic books. They kill the color.

Then, the scariest guy I'd ever seen appeared at the little window.

He was about seven feet tall. He had a big black slouch hat and a loose black coat that reached all the way to the ground. He had a long, really incredibly long, nose. And he had strange eyes. In the shadow of the hat, about all I could see of him was his nose and those eyes! They seemed to be glowing, like a gas flame.

For a long time, the tall scary guy just stood there, not saying a word. I couldn't look away from those eyes. I couldn't feel the floor under my feet. It was hard to breathe.

Finally, he spoke. I could breathe. I felt the floor under my sneakers. The spell was broken.

"Can you fix me a Nuclear Meltdown to go?" the tall scary guy asked.

A Nuclear Meltdown is one of Steve's specialties. It has nine flavors of ice cream, a sliced radish, a peach, four kinds of syrup,

sunflower seeds, bran flakes, a slice of baked ham, and a pickled tomato. The whole thing is served on top of three whole-wheat English muffins and covered with swiss cheese. Just before serving it, you put it under the broiler for a couple of minutes to get the cheese melting. It comes in a big cardboard bucket.

I didn't say a word. I made the Nuclear Meltdown and slid it across the counter, through the little window, to the tall scary guy. He slid a five-dollar bill toward me. I rang up the Nuclear 11 Meltdown and slid his change—five cents—back through the little window. Then he was gone. I felt cold sweat trickle down my back.

Who was that guy?

FOUR

CALM DOWN, NORMAN," Steve said. "You're so excited, I can't understand what you're trying to tell me."

I guess I was excited. The weird guy with the glowing eyes had upset me more than I thought. When Steve walked in with a carton full of dusty princess phones, I started bombarding him with questions about the scary stranger.

Steve fixed me a carrot fizz—that's carrot juice, raspberry syrup, and soda water. As I drank it, I slowed down a bit and asked my questions one at a time.

"You must have seen Lamont Penumbra," Steve said. "He's a regular customer. I'm surprised you never saw him before. He's really a nice fellow. He gives lessons of some sort in a loft over the Puerto Rican restaurant on Washington Street."

"He scared me," I said. "He looked so evil! Did you know that his eyes glow in the dark?"

"Look," Steve said, "it's wrong to judge people by the way they look. Lamont Penumbra is a nice guy, I promise you. In fact, I think we ought to go up to his loft, and I'll introduce you to him. Then you'll see that he's no one to be afraid of."

"Go to his loft? Go where he lives?"

"Sure," Steve said. "I've been up there any number of times. Very often, when he's too busy to come down here, he telephones me, and I deliver a Nuclear Meltdown on my way home after closing time. He has at least one a day. He's a person of taste and culture."

I wasn't at all sure I wanted to go with Steve to visit Lamont Penumbra's loft.

"Let's close up early," Steve said. "I don't think we'll get any more customers tonight. We'll clean up fast and then go over to Lamont Penumbra's."

"Uh . . . I don't think we should just barge in on him," I said. I really didn't want to go and visit that scary guy. I was still feeling a tingling in the soles of my feet, left over from his visit to the Magic Moscow.

"It will be all right," Steve said. "I tell you, he's a very friendly guy."

FIVE

THERE WERE LOTS OF people in the Parthenon Puerto Rican Restaurant. They were talking and laughing and drinking cups of coffee and listening to the juke box and eating sandwiches and plates of roast meat, rice, and inky black beans. Good smells drifted out into the street. It was bright and friendly looking inside the restaurant.

Next to the Parthenon Puerto Rican Restaurant was a doorway. We went in. There was a long flight of dimly lit stairs. It looked as though it went up forever. Everything was greenish and had an underwater look. There were little, dim light bulbs, placed at long intervals along the stairs. They barely gave any light.

We started to climb.

"Are you sure we aren't being rude, coming here without any warning?" I asked.

"It will be all right," Steve said. "You'll see."

We climbed a long way. We passed a few tiny landings with black doors, opening onto apartments or lofts, I supposed. I didn't have the feeling that anybody lived behind those doors. If one had opened suddenly, I would have screamed.

Lamont Penumbra's door was all the way at the top of the stairs. It was a big black-painted door, like the others, but it had neat white-stenciled letters on it: L. PENUMBRA, MYSTIC SEER.

"Mystic seer?" I asked.

"Mystic seer," Steve answered.

He knocked.

"Yes?" I recognized the voice of the guy with the glowing eyes.

"It's Steve Nickelson, from the Magic Moscow—and my helper, Norman Bleistift. We thought we'd drop by to say hello."

"Hello?" said the voice from behind the door.

"Yes—we thought we'd visit you, if that's all right."

"All right," said the voice.

"Uh . . . may we come in?" Steve asked.

"Come in!" the voice said.

Steve pushed the door. It opened into a huge room. It was much, much bigger than my room. It was as big as a basketball court. The room appeared to be mostly empty. It was also mostly dark. At the far end of the room was Lamont Penumbra, sitting under a blue light.

"Kindly approach," he said. "It was nice of you to think of visiting me."

We made our way down the length of the dark room, heading for the blue light and Lamont Penumbra.

When we had arrived at the little table, Lamont Penumbra indicated a couple of chairs, half-visible in the gloom outside the circle of light from his blue lamp. We dragged the chairs closer to the little table and sat down.

Lamont Penumbra was wearing the long black coat and the black broad-brimmed slouch hat he'd been wearing in the street. His face was in shadow, and all we could see was the tip of his enormous nose and the dim blue glow of his eyes.

"You are visitors, is that right?" he asked.

"Yes," Steve said, "visitors."

"You are not seekers?"

"Seekers?" Steve asked. "What's that?"

I was impressed by the way that Steve didn't seem nervous at all. I, myself, was plenty scared of Lamont Penumbra. Steve's idea that visiting him would help me get over being scared was not working out.

"Seekers," Lamont Penumbra said. "Seekers after mystical truths, students of the occult,

persons desiring to learn the ancient wisdom—
you're none of those?''

"No," Steve said. "We just wanted to visit."

"In that case," said Lamont Penumbra, "let's
get some light on the subject."

He flipped a switch, and ceiling lights came
on—regular ones. The blue gloom was gone.
Lamont Penumbra also took off his hat and long
black coat, revealing himself as bald and very tall
and skinny. He was wearing a yellow T-shirt with
a picture of a wave on it and the slogan *I'd Rather
Be Surfing.*

"You guys want a cup of tea?" Lamont
Penumbra asked.

SIX

MR. PENUMBRA," STEVE
began.

"Call me Lamont."

"Lamont," Steve continued, "Norman and I
were talking about you a while ago, and I was
telling him that I never did know just what it is
you do."

"Do?"

"Yes. I mean, what's a mystic seer?"

"Oh, you mean my profession," Lamont
Penumbra said. "Well, as a mystic seer I do a
number of things. I cast horoscopes, read palms,
read tarot cards, give mystical advice, and answer
questions. I can also chase ghosts, if you have
them, and tell things about what will happen to
you by feeling the bumps on your head."

"So you're a fortune-teller," Steve said.

"That's it," Lamont Penumbra said.

"I never believed in any of that stuff, myself," Steve said.

"Neither do I," Lamont Penumbra said.

"You don't believe in it?" Steve asked. "You mean you're a fake?"

"Well—sort of," Lamont Penumbra said.

"Isn't that dishonest?" Steve asked.

"Not really," Lamont Penumbra said. "I honestly tell my customers what they want to hear. I try not to tell any big lies. The only thing that's a tiny bit dishonest is that I don't tell them that the horoscopes and so forth are nonsense. Of course, if they were to ask me, I'd tell them—but they never ask."

"Mr. Penumbra," I said.

"Call me Lamont."

"Lamont." I went on, "If you are a fake fortune-teller, how are you able to make your eyes glow like they did when you came to the Magic Moscow earlier? I was really scared."

"There are tricks to every trade," Lamont Penumbra said. "The idea isn't so much to scare you as to impress people. I wouldn't be very good as a mystic seer if I couldn't impress people."

By this time, I wasn't feeling very afraid of Lamont Penumbra at all. He was just a nice middle-aged hippie. The teakettle began to whistle, and he busied himself making a pot of tea for us. It smelled of mint.

22   "This is very interesting," Steve said. "I've never met a mystic seer before. Is it the same as a wizard?"

"I only wish it was," Lamont Penumbra said. "A wizard! That's what I started out to be. Somehow everything I studied in the wizard line turned out to be either a fraud or something which did not work at all. I always wanted to be a real magician, but I was never able to learn any real magic. I'm not even sure if there is such a thing anymore. So I make my living by telling people that they are going to be rich and happy by feeling the bumps on their heads. On Saturday nights, I put on a gypsy suit and tell fortunes in the restaurant downstairs in exchange for a free meal. It's really very depressing when I think about it."

Lamont Penumbra looked very depressed as he sipped his mint-flavored tea.

"I didn't mean to bring up any sensitive subjects," Steve said. "I hope you aren't mad at us."

"No, no! Not at all," Lamont Penumbra said. "It's really very nice to have visitors who aren't interested in having their fortunes told. Everybody who comes up here wants me to do their horoscope and tell them they're going to be rich and happy. It's nice to have regular visitors for a change."

"You know," Steve said, "I purchased a large private library recently that had a lot of magical books in it. I, myself, am only interested in comic books and science fiction. The magical books look very old. Maybe you'd like to have them."

"That's very kind of you," Lamont Penumbra said.

"I'll have Norman bring them up tomorrow," Steve said.

SEVEN

THE NEXT DAY, STEVE gave me a carton of old books to take to Lamont Penumbra's loft.

I climbed the stairs. They were just as dark by day as they had been the night before. When I came to Lamont Penumbra's door, with the stenciled white letters, L. PENUMBRA, MYSTIC SEER, I knocked.

"Yes?"

"It's me," I said. "Norman Bleistift. I was here last night with Steve Nickelson."

"Here?" asked the voice from behind the door.

"Yes," I said, "we were here. I've got the books Steve told you about."

"Books?"

"Yes. May I come in?"

"Come in."

I pushed the door open with the carton of

books. I wasn't surprised to see that Lamont Penumbra's loft was just as dark as it had been the previous night. There he was, wearing his black hat and coat, sitting by the blue light.

"Approach," he said.

I approached, "Look, Mr. Penumbra. . . ."

"Call me Lamont."

"Look, Lamont, it's just me, Norman. I've got the magical books Steve promised you. You don't have to go through this whole routine with the blue light and all."

"You *are* all alone?" Lamont Penumbra asked. "This crummy blue light is ruining my eyesight. I wouldn't want a potential customer to come in here and catch me out of character. Now, let's have a look at the books."

The books in the carton were all pretty old. The oldest-looking ones were stubby and fat, printed on thick yellow paper that was wavy like potato chips and bound in smooth white leather that was all smudged and black at the corners and on the spine. There were other old books, bound in red and black leather and stamped in gold. There were quite a few books in the carton.

"Look at this," Lamont Penumbra said. "This is some pretty good stuff!" He pulled out one of the volumes. "*Malleus Malificarum!* An oldie but a goodie! Here's another classic, *Die Magie als*

Naturwissenschaft. And what have we here?" Lamont Penumbra was obviously having a good time. "Here's one I never heard of, *Natura Magicum Phantomium,* and another, *The Experiments of Istvan of Budapest.* These are all good books! And here's the good old *Sorcerer's Guide!*

"Norman, please tell Steve that I am very grateful for this box of books. They're really wonderful! I'll come down and thank him in person later—but now, if you'll excuse me, I want to start reading some of these right away."

With that, Lamont Penumbra began diving into first one book and then another, mumbling and licking his fingers as he leafed through pages. He'd read a little of one book and then grab another, riffling through it until he found something interesting, and then grab another, and so on. He took no notice of me. After a while, I tiptoed out and quietly closed the door. He was still flipping through one book after another and mumbling to himself.

I went back to the Magic Moscow and told Steve that Lamont Penumbra was having a good time with the books he had sent. Then I went in the back and put a few pounds of carrots through the juicer for the noon rush.

EIGHT

STEVE WAS RUNNING A special on The Hungarian Boy Scout Lunch. It cost a dollar seventy-five. It consisted of two cold, cooked hot dogs, two slices of rye bread, a chocolate bar, and a pack of cigarettes. The idea was that you took it with you to the park and had a picnic. "This is what Hungarian Boy Scouts always take with them on hikes," Steve said.

It didn't seem likely that all Hungarian Boy Scouts smoked cigarettes. Also, it didn't seem like much of a lunch to me. Apparently, nobody thought so either, because Steve hardly sold any all day.

Steve couldn't understand it. He had about three dozen Hungarian Boy Scout Lunches all made up and standing on the counter in brown paper bags. In the end, Steve made me eat Hungarian Boy Scout Lunches all that week.

Edward refused to even sniff them. Steve smoked the cigarettes.

The weather got warmer, and the ice-cream business picked up. There were lots of people out strolling at night, and there were long lines under the yellow fluorescent lights.

It was a normal week.

We hadn't seen Lamont Penumbra for quite a few days after I had taken him the box of magical books.

He turned up on a warm afternoon. He was wearing his black coat and hat as usual. There was sweat dripping from the end of his nose.

Lamont Penumbra pushed five fat candles through the little window. "Take these," he said, "and put them in a circle on the floor; light them at midnight. I've got a great surprise for you." Then he hurried off, his black coat flapping behind him.

Steve put the candles on the shelf where he keeps the paper napkins and straws. That night, at five minutes to midnight, after closing time, he put each candle on a paper plate, stuck to it with a little drip of wax, and lighted them in a circle on the floor.

The phone rang. It was Lamont Penumbra. "Did you light the candles?" he asked.

"We just lighted them," I said.

"Okay. Good. Now, just sit down and watch

the middle of the circle," Lamont Penumbra said over the phone. "You're going to see something really fantastic in a few minutes."

I told Steve what Lamont Penumbra had said. We pulled up chairs and sat down, watching the flickering candles.

Nothing happened.

About fifteen minutes went by. The candles flickered. The refrigerators hummed. Edward snored. Steve smoked cigarettes left over from the Hungarian Boy Scout Lunches.

The candles were about a quarter burned. They were smoking a lot.

"Maybe we ought to turn out the lights," I said.

"Okay," Steve said, and he did it.

Neither of us said anything. We sat in chairs and waited for Lamont Penumbra's fantastic trick to come off.

It never did.

After about a half-hour, when the candles were burned halfway down, the phone rang. It was Lamont again.

This time Steve answered. "Did you see anything?" Lamont Penumbra asked.

"Like what?" Steve wanted to know.

"Anything unusual," Lamont Penumbra said.

"No," Steve said, "we just watched the candles. It was very restful."

"Oh, rats!" Lamont Penumbra said. "You mean you didn't see anything amazing? Anything magical?"

"No," Steve said. "But I did have an amazing thought."

"Like a vision? What was it?" Lamont Penumbra asked.

"Well, I'm going to get those red glass things with candles in them and put them on all the tables," Steve said. "Then, at night we'll light them. You can get them with insect-repellent candles, so they'll keep the mosquitoes away, besides making the place look very nice."

There was a long silence on the phone. Finally, Lamont Penumbra said, "Look, I'm very depressed. Do you think you might come up here and maybe bring me a Nuclear Meltdown? I need cheering up."

"Will do," Steve said and hung up.

NINE

I HAD NEVER ACTUALLY watched anyone eat a Nuclear Meltdown. It was a spectacular sight. Lamont Penumbra dug into the gigantic, gloppy, gooey mess with enthusiasm.

Steve and I munched on the last two Hungarian Boy Scout Lunches, which we had brought along. I was glad they were the last. The cold hot dogs were all shriveled up and nasty looking after a whole week in the back of the refrigerator.

As he mopped up the last of the Nuclear Meltdown, Lamont Penumbra said, "Well, it happened again—rather, it didn't happen again. It's the story of my life."

"I don't quite follow," Steve said. "What are you talking about?"

"The experiment," Lamont Penumbra said, "with the five candles. I was sure it would work. I

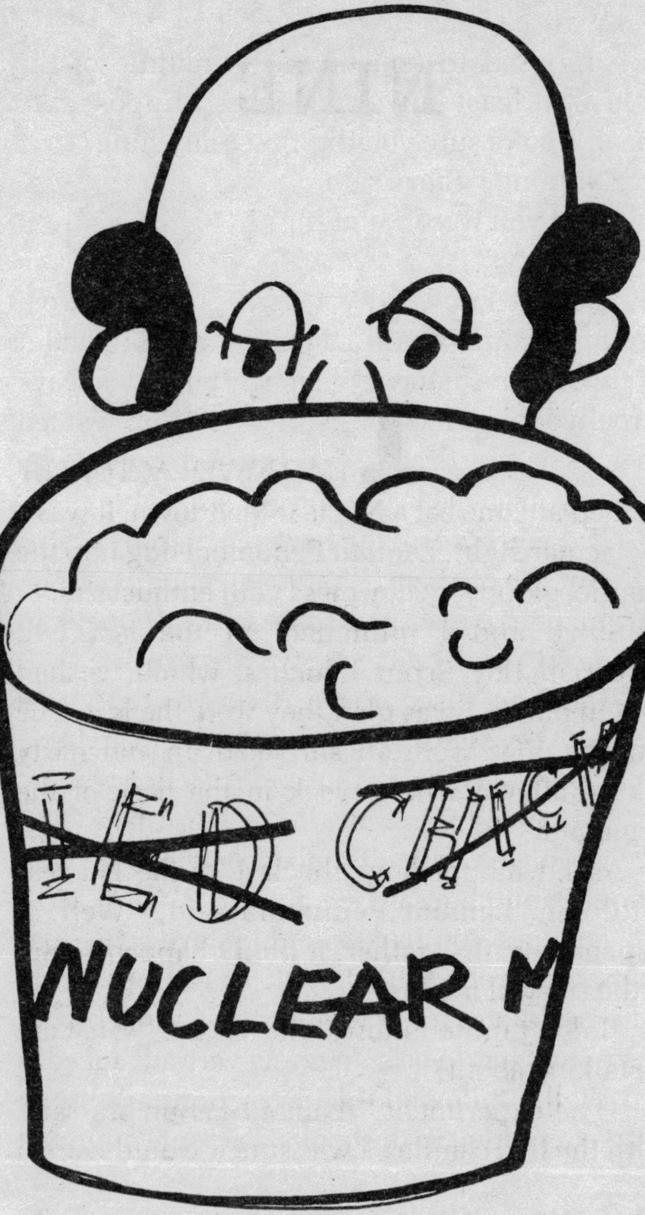
NUCLEAR M

was supposed to appear in the middle of the circle—at least my image was supposed to appear. You're sure you didn't see anything?"

"Nothing," Steve said.

"And you were watching?"

"Intently."

"I don't know why I don't just give up," Lamont Penumbra said. "I really thought I had it this time. Some of those old magic books you gave me really looked like the genuine article. I wanted you to see the first real magic I'd ever done, because you gave me the books."

35

"Did you read all the books?" I asked.

"Not all of them," Lamont Penumbra said, "but the ones I read had some fantastic spells in them. I can't understand why it didn't work."

"Don't get discouraged," Steve said. "Magic must be very hard to do; otherwise, everybody would do it. Maybe you picked a spell that was too difficult, or maybe you made a little mistake."

"Or maybe I just don't have any real talent," Lamont Penumbra said.

"I'm sure you have talent," Steve said, "but you picked a very difficult trick. I mean, appearing in the middle of a circle of candles three blocks away—that has to be something very advanced."

"Well, I followed the instructions exactly as they were written in the book," Lamont Penumbra said. "The only thing I didn't have was powdered unicorn horn to make the candles with, so I used moth flakes. Do you suppose a little thing like that could make the spell go wrong?"

"Of course!" Steve said. "That has to be it. You can't work with inferior materials. That's why the olive milk shake I invented last month was a failure—I used canned olives. You have to get good stuff, if you want good results."

"Maybe you're right," Lamont Penumbra said, "but then things are just as hopeless. You have no idea how many ingredients are simply impossible to get. Unicorn horn is just one of them. The witchcraft supply house in New York City doesn't have half the things I need."

"Aren't there any easy spells in any of the books?" I asked. "I mean, aren't there any tricks that don't require hard-to-get stuff?" I had always thought that magicians, if they really existed, could make things happen just by saying magic words or maybe waving a magic wand. I never knew they needed unicorn horn or anything like that.

"There are some easy spells," Lamont Penumbra said, "but they aren't very interesting. For example, there's a spell for making a razor blade last twice as long as normal. And there's a spell for ensuring that no one will steal your shoes while you're asleep, and one against people putting poison in your well, and one against having a horseshoe fall on your head from a great height. You see? Spells like that may have been useful at one time, but they aren't much fun."

"Isn't there something sort of in-between?" Steve asked.

"Well, I found one spell that was kind of cute," Lamont Penumbra said, "and it doesn't require any special equipment or ingredients. It's one that makes a person able to summon the ghost of a famous person from history."

"Which famous person?" Steve asked.

"The spell doesn't say," Lamont Penumbra said, "and . . . I just remembered, there's a catch to that one. It only works on people less than sixty inches in height. I'm six foot six—that's seventy-eight inches."

"I'm six feet tall myself," Steve said, "but Norman might be less than sixty inches. Can the spell work for someone else?"

"I suppose so," Lamont Penumbra said. "How tall are you, Norman?"

"I don't know exactly," I said. "I've been doing a lot of growing lately."

"Stand up straight against this wall," Lamont Penumbra said. He made a mark on the wall with a pencil. Then he rummaged around and found a ruler. "Rats!" he said. "I make this fifty-nine and seven-eighths inches. I don't think it will work—that's pretty close to sixty."

"But you measured him with his shoes on," Steve said. "Does the book say whether the spell will work on someone less than sixty inches tall with his shoes on or less than sixty inches tall with his shoes off? Besides, Norman is an eighth of an inch under the mark, even with his shoes on. Let's give the spell a try."

"All right," Lamont Penumbra said, "but I don't expect it to work."

Lamont Penumbra had me take my shoes off, just to be on the safe side, and stand in the middle of the room.

"Now this won't hurt a bit," Lamont Penumbra said. "You don't have to do anything. Just stand there with your eyes closed and think pleasant thoughts. While you do that, I am going to go into a mystic trance, and then I'll throw a sort of fit. Don't be alarmed, or take any notice of what I do. Just stand there, thinking pleasant thoughts. After a while, you will feel the irresistible urge to bark like a dog, mew like a cat, neigh like a horse, honk like a goose, hiss like a snake, and so forth. Just go ahead and do those things—don't be afraid that you'll appear foolish. You won't appear any more foolish than I will. When I say 'stop' you will stop barking, mewing, neighing, honking, hissing, and so on. Then the ghost of a famous person from history will appear and talk to us. Is that okay with you?"

I said it was.

"You're doing this very well, Lamont," Steve said.

"Thank you," Lamont Penumbra said. "Now, let's get started."

I stood in the middle of the room with my shoes off. I tried to think pleasant thoughts. The best one I could come up with was being in a rented rowboat in the little lake in North Hudson Park. That's something I often think about just as I fall asleep.

Meanwhile, Lamont Penumbra went into a mystic trance. At least, I suppose he did—my eyes were closed.

Then he had his fit, just as he said he would. It was hard to keep my eyes closed. I really wanted to peek and see what he was doing. I could hear him thumping around the room and muttering strange things. Later, Steve told me that he had been hopping around the room on one foot—backward.

He was mumbling something like, "Waka hakakabakka kawakaka baka waka waka hakakawaka."

Everything went according to plan—except

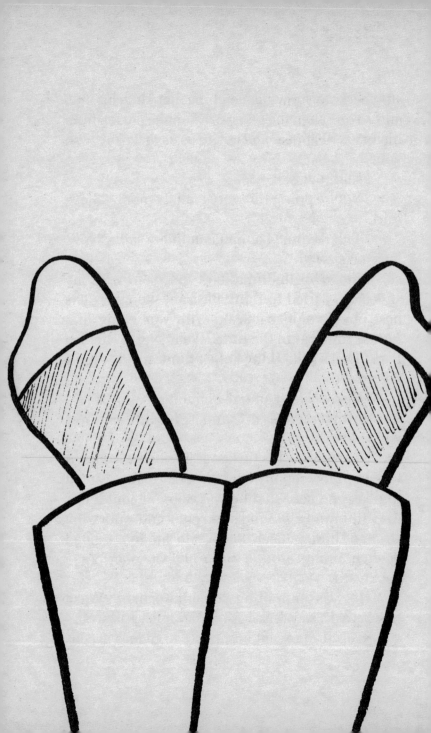

that I did not bark, nor mew, nor neigh. Neither did I honk or hiss like a snake. Mostly I just stood there feet bare and eyes closed. It must have gone on for half an hour.

"Did you feel anything?" Lamont Penumbra asked me.

"No." I was embarrassed. I felt sorry for Lamont Penumbra. I wished that I had felt an irresistible urge to bark at least once. But, I hadn't felt a thing, except bored and foolish.

"Oh, rats! Double rats!" Lamont Penumbra said. "I'm so depressed! I don't want to live anymore!"

I felt terrible. I felt as though I had let Lamont Penumbra down. "I really tried," I said.

"We know you did," Steve said, "but it's getting late. Maybe you should go home before your parents get worried. I'll stay with Lamont and make sure he doesn't hurt himself. Maybe we'll go out for a pizza."

As I left the loft, I could hear Lamont Penumbra saying, "Rats! Rats! Double rats!" and Steve saying, "You like anchovies?"

TEN

MY PARENTS ARE LATE-
movie freaks. They're always up until at least two
in the morning, so it's no big deal when I come
home from the Magic Moscow after midnight—in
the summer, that is.

They were watching the movie where
Anthony Quinn plays an Eskimo when I got home.
I said hello to them and went downstairs to my
room.

Arthur was sleeping in the middle of my bed.
I picked him up and put him on a chair. He half
woke up and gave me one raspy lick. Then he
started snoring again. He's the only cat I know of
who snores.

I kicked my shoes off.

In the middle of unbuttoning my shirt, I stood
in the middle of my room and closed my eyes.

Without meaning to, or wanting to, I barked

once—then a lot of times. Then I miaowed, whinnied, honked like a goose, and hissed like a snake.

"Stop all that noise and go to bed!" my father shouted from upstairs.

"That was the silliest performance I've ever seen," someone else said. There was someone in my room!

Arthur was wide awake and staring at a point behind me as though he were looking at a ghost.

I felt a tingling all over my body. Lamont Penumbra's spell had worked after all! It had worked! Somehow the working of the spell had been delayed for a while—and now, there was a ghost in my room! Behind me was the ghost of some famous person from history. I was scared. Arthur was making a low moaning noise, and all his fur was standing straight up.

"Are you a ghost?" I asked unsteadily.

"I am a ghost," the voice behind me said, "a spirit summoned here by your incantation."

"Are you the ghost of a famous person from history?" I asked.

"Yes," said the voice. "I am the ghost of Alexander Hamilton, first secretary of the treasury of the United States. I was killed in a duel in 1804, just across the town line in Weehawken."

I pulled myself together. Alexander Hamilton

wasn't scary. I'd read about him in school. I turned slowly and faced the ghost.

Never having seen a ghost before, I didn't know quite what to expect. What I saw was quite a surprise. For one thing, it wasn't someone wrapped in a white sheet or glowing like a neon light. What I saw was a short guy, with a snub nose and tangled gray hair. He was wearing some kind of fur thing over his shoulders, and his arms were bare. He was sort of dark in coloring and had big muscles. On his head, the ghost had a leather helmet with a point on top, and he was wearing a sort of short skirt made of plates of iron. On his feet he had rags wrapped with rope, and he was holding a big sword.

"You're not Alexander Hamilton!" I said, before I knew what I was doing. I had seen a picture of Alexander Hamilton in my history book, and he didn't look anything like this.

"No," the ghost said. "In fact, I am not Alexander Hamilton. I just said that for a joke. The truth is, I am really the ghost of Frank Sinatra."

"I've seen Frank Sinatra on television," I said, "and you're not him. Besides, I don't think he's even dead."

"Look," the ghost said, "why did you summon me if you just want to argue?"

"I don't want to argue," I said, "and it wasn't

really me that summoned you. It was this guy, Lamont Penumbra . . . who are you really?''

"Look at me!" the ghost said. "Do you really mean to say that you don't know who I am?"

I looked at the ghost. He looked pretty scruffy. Also, he smelled of horses. I never knew that you could smell a ghost. "I give up," I said. "Who are you?"

"I am Attila!" the ghost said.

I knew who that was! "No kidding?" I said. "Are you really Attila, the Hun, the Scourge of God? The guy who subjugated Europe in the fifth century? Who engaged in all kinds of battles, raised huge armies, and rode all over the place, putting cities and people to the torch?" This had been one of my favorite parts of the history book.

"Well, to be absolutely truthful," the ghost said, "no, I'm not. If you want to know, I'm Attila's brother, Bleda. Someone accidentally chopped my head off with a sword in the year 445. It still comes off—want to see?" The ghost made a gesture, offering to remove his head for me.

"No thanks," I said, "please keep your head on." I was surprised to find that I wasn't too terribly scared of this ghost, but I really didn't want to see him take his head off.

"You can call me Attila," he said. "People used to call me Attila—but they didn't call me Attila the Hun."

"What did they call you?" I asked.

"They called me . . . Attila the Pun!" the ghost said. "When is a door not a door? When it's ajar! When is a door ready to eat? When it's jammed! Why did the toast rise to the ceiling? Because butter flies! What do jokers eat for breakfast? Puns and coffee!" Then he started laughing and staggered around the room, howling and slapping his legs with his hands. He really thought he was a riot. All of a sudden, I was sure I knew why he had gotten his head chopped off.

I also was worried that all the laughing would bring my parents down. Somehow I didn't want to try to explain to them what a fifth century idiot was doing in my basement after midnight.

"Look, Attila," I said, "can you . . . uh . . . move about? Go from place to place?"

"Why not?" the Hun said.

"Well, I want you to come with me," I said. "I want you to meet this guy, Lamont Penumbra, the one who summoned you. He'll be very happy to see that his spell worked."

"Spell!" Attila said. "Railroad crossing: Look out for the cars—Can you spell it without any 'r's?"

"I—T," I said.

"Oh," Attila said.

"Now, look," I told the Hunnish clown, "we

have to climb out this window. I'm going to turn out the lights so my parents will think I'm asleep."

"Lights!" Attila said. "Do you know how many Visigoths it takes to screw in a new candle?"

"Tell me later," I said and pushed the giggling ghost out the window up onto the sidewalk.

ELEVEN

GETTING ATTILA THROUGH the streets of Hoboken was something of a problem. He kept wanting to stop and look at things and tell stale jokes. For example, he went into a bar and said, "Hey! Do you serve spirits here?"

Apparently everybody could see him, not just me. He didn't look particularly ghostly, just messy and dirty.

I knew where to find Steve and Lamont Penumbra. They would be at Kevin Schwartz's Pizzeria. It was Steve's favorite place, and he often went there for three or four pizzas after closing the Magic Moscow.

When we got to the pizzeria, I could see Steve and Lamont Penumbra through the window. They were sharing Kevin Schwartz's super special thirty-six-inch pizza. I dragged Attila into the restaurant.

"Hey!" he said. "An Italian restaurant! Do they serve spookghetti here?"

"Steve," I said, "we've got a problem."

Lamont Penumbra almost choked on his pizza when I told him who Attila was. At first he didn't believe me. He thought that Attila was just some weirdo, and that I was trying to play a joke on him. As I said, Attila didn't look much like a ghost—at least not anybody's idea of a ghost. Finally, they began to believe me, because, as Steve said, it would be hard for anyone to get to be as dirty as Attila in less than fifteen hundred years.

When it finally sank in that this was a ghost of an almost famous person from history and that the spell had actually worked, Lamont Penumbra was so happy that he sort of went crazy.

"It worked! It worked! The spell worked!" he shouted. Lamont Penumbra got up and started capering around.

"Take it easy!" Steve said. "Don't lose your head."

That was the wrong thing to say. "I can take my head off," Attila said. "Want to see?"

"NO!" we all shouted.

It turned out that ghosts don't actually eat, but they enjoy sniffing food. After we got Lamont Penumbra somewhat calmed down, we ordered a second super special thirty-six-inch pizza for

Attila to inhale over. He liked it very much and said that pizza had been improved a lot since his day.

Attila caused a certain amount of stir in the pizzeria; not because he was a ghost—only we knew that—but because he was so weird looking. Fortunately, Kevin Schwartz is a good guy, or he might have asked us to leave.

Steve was very impressed to be sitting at a table with Attila the Pun. "I always liked your brother, the Hun," he said.

"Sure," Attila said. "Everybody likes him— but it's not true that he had a great sense of humor. You probably heard that he did, didn't you?"

"Mostly I heard that he rode around on a shaggy pony and everybody was afraid of him," Steve said.

"Well, that part is true," Attila the Pun said, "but any jokes you may have heard that he supposedly told were probably mine. For example, there's this famous one: How do you find your dog if he's lost in the woods?"

None of us knew.

"You put your ear to a tree and listen to the bark," Attila the Pun said. "Now that's one that everybody claims was told by my brother, the Hun—but it's my joke. I've been very ill-treated by history."

"That's a shame," Lamont Penumbra said.

"It is," Attila said, "and the rotten part of it is, when you're dead, you can't do anything about it. Live people can say or write anything, and you just have to put up with it. That's why I'm not so famous, and my brother is."

"What's it like, being dead?" I asked.

"Oh, it's nice," Attila said, "but it gets boring after a few hundred years. I'm glad you summoned me. If you're not going to finish that root beer, I'd like to sniff it."

"I guess things were very different when you were alive," Steve said.

"I'll say," Attila said. "I traveled all over with my brother, and I never came across pizza like this. I wish I could eat it. You guys are living at the right time, that's for sure."

It was interesting, sitting around with a ghost from the fifth century. Of course, it was hard to get Attila to tell us things about when he was alive. Mostly he wanted to tell jokes. I was surprised to learn that all the elephant jokes the kids tell in school were already popular back then.

About the time Attila was telling his fiftieth elephant joke—the one that goes, "How do you know if there's an elephant in your tent?"—I started yawning.

"Say, it's pretty late," Steve said. "Norman,

you'd better go home and get some sleep."

"Okay," Attila said. "Let's go, Norman."

"Wait a minute," I said. "Is he going to come home with me?"

"Of course," Attila said, "I have to stay with you. You're the one who summoned me."

"I keep telling you," I said, "it was really Lamont Penumbra who summoned you. I think you ought to go to his place." I just didn't want to have to deal with explaining Attila to my parents. They'd given me enough trouble about the moose head—and Attila really *did* have fleas.

"Well, if you say so," Attila said.

"Uh, do you . . . do ghosts . . . sleep, or what?" Lamont Penumbra asked.

"No, ghosts don't sleep," Attila said. "Mostly, I pace up and down and talk to myself; I sing Hunnish songs and whack things with my sword all night. But you go ahead and sleep. I'll be fine by myself."

"Right," I said, "I'll be going now."

"Me, too," Steve said. "Let's all meet for breakfast at the Magic Moscow."

"Fair enough," Attila said, "I'll go with Lamont. By the way, do you know the difference between a rain cloud and an Ostrogoth with his toe cut off?"

Nobody said anything. It was maybe the two-hundredth riddle of the evening.

"One pours with rain, and the other roars with pain," Attila said.

"Good night, Attila," I said.

"Good night, Attila," Steve said.

"Good night! Don't let the bedbugs bite!" Attila said.

TWELVE

I USUALLY EAT BREAKfast at the Magic Moscow during the summer. Steve doesn't serve breakfast to the public. The Magic Moscow opens at lunchtime. My mother hates to cook breakfast, so she's happy that I get fed at work. I like to eat there because Steve is very good at experimental breakfasts. For example, he makes scrambled eggs with chili peppers, toasted carrot cereal, and avocado pancakes— none of which I ever get at home.

On the morning following Attila's appearance, I arrived at the Magic Moscow bright and early. Lamont Penumbra was already there, having a coffee omelet. It was the first time I had ever seen Lamont Penumbra outside his loft without his black hat and coat. He was wearing a pair of blue jeans and a T-shirt with the three little pigs on it. He looked as if he hadn't had much sleep.

"Hi, Norman," he said. "I haven't had much sleep."

"Eat your eggs," Steve said. "They're full of caffeine."

Attila was wandering around behind the counter, sniffing his breakfast. "Hey!" he said to me. "This is a soda fountain! You work here—do you know how to make an elephant float?"

"Tie little water wings on him?" I asked.

"No," Attila said. "To make an elephant float, you need two scoops of ice cream, some root beer, an elephant, and a really huge blender."

"So how's everything?" I asked Lamont Penumbra, sitting down at the table. Steve went behind the counter to make me a bean-sprout omelet, my current favorite.

"That ghost is murder," Lamont Penumbra said. "All night he was stomping up and down, singing horrible songs in Hun, or whatever his native language is. And he told jokes to himself, and he laughed at them. I counted four hundred and fifty elephant jokes before I finally fell asleep from sheer exhaustion. And he whacked stuff with his sword. He whacked most of the stuffing out of my sofa. I can't stand another night with him in my place. What's more, I keep scratching. Is it possible to catch fleas from a ghost?"

"It's hard to string a violin," Attila said. "It

takes guts." Then he stuck his nose up the spout of the soft ice-cream machine.

Steve brought me my bean-sprout omelet. "That Attila's a real problem," he said. "The only one who likes him without any reservations is Edward."

Edward, the Malamute dog, had taken a great fancy to the Hunnish slob and was following him everywhere, with his tail wagging.

"It's not that Attila isn't a nice fellow in an ancient, moronic sort of way—it's just that he's very hard to have around," Steve whispered.

"So what we wanted to know, Norman . . ." Lamont Penumbra whispered.

" . . . is, what are you going to do with him?" Steve continued.

"Me?" I asked, astonished. "Why me? What's this got to do with me?"

"Well, Attila thinks you're responsible for him," Steve said.

"He says that no matter who started the spell, you were the one who summoned him," Lamont Penumbra said.

"He says he's your responsibility, and you have to decide what to do with him," Steve said. "We all discussed it before breakfast."

"Thanks a lot," I said. "I'm just a kid, and you guys are trying to fob off the responsibility for a

Hun who's been dead for fifteen hundred years on me. That's really nice."

"Norman, it's just that he's making me crazy," Lamont Penumbra said.

"He says he doesn't have to listen to us," Steve said. "He says you're the only mortal he has to take any account of."

"Talk to him," Lamont Penumbra said. "Tell him he can't stay in my loft any more."

Just then, Bruce the Milkman arrived.

"Hey! A milkman!" Attila said. "What has only one horn and gives milk? Give up? A milk truck!"

"Who's this guy?" Bruce asked. "He looks like Attila the Hun."

"Typical," Attila said. "Say, milkman, why does the ocean roar?"

"I don't know," Bruce the Milkman said. "Why does the ocean roar?"

"You'd roar too if you had crabs on your bottom," Attila said.

"Say, this guy's pretty funny," Bruce the Milkman said. "Is he going to be performing here all the time?" Bruce carried the last of the empties out to his wagon, clucked to his horse, Cheryl, and drove off.

"Talk to him," Steve whispered.

"Um . . . Attila," I said.

"Right. . . . Did you see that guy's horse? How many legs does a horse have?"

"Four," I said.

"Wrong! Six! Forelegs in front and two in back."

"Attila, how long are you planning to stay?" I asked.

"How long?"

"Yes," I said, "I mean, don't you have things to do? Don't you have to get back to being . . . uh . . . dead?"

"Not really," Attila said. "Don't you worry, I can stay for a long time."

"Uh . . . you don't want to go back to being . . ."

"Dead? No, I like it here. I'm going to sniff some more of that pizza tonight."

Attila went into the storeroom to sniff the jars of cherries in Red Dye Number Two that Steve kept there. I went back to the table where Steve and Lamont Penumbra were sitting.

"He says he likes it here," I said. "He says he likes the way the food smells. He says he doesn't have to go back for a long time."

"What are we going to do with him?" Lamont Penumbra said. "He's not staying at my place anymore, that's final."

"Lamont, isn't there a spell for sending him back where he came from?"

"You think I didn't look that up at three this morning?" Lamont Penumbra asked. "Of course there's a spell, but the ghost has to be willing to go. You see, it works like this. Most ghosts want to go back. They like it there. When you're a ghost, you sort of stay in a time and place comparable to where you were when you were alive. So Attila doesn't feel like going back to what must be a bunch of fifth-century Huns, where the pizza isn't any good. Sooner or later he'll go back by himself or I can cast a spell and send him—but until then, he's with us."

Attila came out of the storeroom. "You know what you get if you cross a cat and a lemon?" he asked. "A sourpuss!"

THIRTEEN

IT WAS UP TO ME TO figure out what to do with Attila. Steve and Lamont Penumbra didn't seem to have any ideas. Attila probably never had an idea in his life—or after.

I went and got a chocolate-dipped frozen carrot from the freezer and munched it while I thought things over. Meanwhile, Steve and Lamont Penumbra sat around, looking bewildered, and Attila sniffed this and that and occasionally told a joke.

Then it came to me! A great idea! If it worked, it would be one of the great ideas of all time.

"Look, Steve," I said, "you always worry that someone will break into the Magic Moscow at night and maybe steal Edward, right?"

"Well, yes," Steve said. "Edward is a valuable dog—and most of my comics are here, too. I was thinking that maybe I should get a burglar alarm."

"How about something better than a burglar alarm?" I said. "How about a real live—or in this case, a real dead—night watchman?"

"You mean Attila?" Lamont Penumbra asked. "It won't work. Attila doesn't like to be alone."

"He wouldn't be alone," I said. "Edward would be with him. Edward likes him."

"That's because Edward doesn't understand his jokes," Lamont Penumbra said.

"It might be all right," Steve said.

"Of course it will," I said. "Attila doesn't eat food—he only sniffs it—so it won't cost anything to keep him."

"But during the day, Attila will drive the customers crazy by telling jokes," Steve said. "How will we get him to agree to sort of stay out of sight during business hours?"

"I've thought of that, too," I said. "If Attila agrees, I think there's a way to keep him happy, and everybody else, too. Will you give my idea a try?"

"Sure," Steve said, "it's the only idea we've got."

"Okay," I said, "I'm going to have a talk with Attila now, and if he agrees, we'll give my idea a try."

FOURTEEN

ATTILA AGREED. I GOT busy making posters and putting them up all over Hoboken.

The posters invited everyone in town to come to the Magic Moscow that night for free toasted carrot sandwiches and goat's milk malteds and to hear a concert of recorded jazz music and a surprise "live" entertainer.

The entertainer was Attila, of course. He spent the whole day in the storeroom, practicing his material—as if he hadn't had enough practice in fifteen hundred years. We closed the Magic Moscow for an hour after the suppertime rush and arranged all the chairs and tables so the people would be able to see the stage. The stage was a space in front of the counter lit by a spotlight I got from my room—something I had found in the street and repaired.

It was a Friday night, and we got a pretty good crowd. In fact, the place was just about full. Steve had added a black clip-on bow tie to the white soda jerk uniform he always wore. He stood at the door and shook hands with everybody as they came in. Lamont Penumbra and I served the toasted carrot sandwiches and goat's milk malteds, and we changed the records on Steve's record player. He had selected a bunch of boogie-woogie piano records for the evening, and the people at the tables were tapping their feet and having a good time.

Then, we turned down the lights and switched on the spotlight. Steve stepped into the circle of light and said, "Ladies and gentlemen, the Magic Moscow is proud to present a great comedian, the late Attila the Pun!"

Attila came out of the storeroom. He was sweating. "Good evening, ladies and germs," he said. "Did you hear about the two cannonballs? They got married and had B.B.'s!"

The audience laughed.

"Hey! I'm a ghost, you know?" Attila said. He was getting comfortable. "You know what ghosts eat for breakfast? Ghost toasties! Hey! Do you know what ghosts like to do at the amusement park? They ride the roller ghoster! Hey! Are you all enjoying your ghost milk malteds? Hey! You know

what a spirit on guard duty says? Who ghost there? Hey!''

The audience loved him. It turned out that fifth-century Hun humor really goes over well in Hoboken. Attila told jokes for almost an hour. Finally Steve had to lead him off, saying, "Save something for next Friday night."

"I've got a million of them!" Attila said.

Attila's act at the Magic Moscow is the biggest thing in Hoboken. Some Friday nights we can hardly get all the people inside. Steve is happy because he doesn't have to worry about someone breaking in at night and stealing Edward, and he likes playing the old jazz records for the people who come to laugh at Attila's jokes.

Attila is happy. He was so grateful to me for thinking up my great idea that he is letting me keep his sword for him. It looks really good, Attila's genuine fifth-century Hun sword, hanging from the antlers of my stuffed moose.